# ROBIN THE OUTLAW

*Robin of Locksley was a Saxon gentleman*

# CLASSIC FABLES AND LEGENDS

# THE ADVENTURES OF ROBIN HOOD

Robin the Outlaw

Little John • The Silver Arrow

*Retold by John Grant*

*Illustrated by Victor G Ambrus*

# CONTENTS

Robin of Locksley was a Saxon gentleman. He lived long ago, near the town of Nottingham, on the edge of the great and ancient forest of Sherwood.

The King of England was Richard, called Lionheart. He was a Norman, as were most English noblemen of the time. The ordinary people were Saxons, and many were treated harshly by their cruel and greedy Norman lords. King Richard, who should have punished the wrongdoers, was far away, fighting in the Holy Land. In his place he had left his brother, Prince John... the cruellest and greediest Norman of all.

Early one summer's day, Robin of Locksley left his home, Locksley Hall. Not all Normans were wicked, and one of Robin's friends was a young Norman lady, Marian Fitzwalter. She was returning from a visit, and her way led through Sherwood Forest.

The forest was a dangerous place, where travellers risked attack and robbery by outlaws and brigands. Robin had agreed to meet Marian and her servants, and escort them on the last few miles to her father's house. Shouldering his longbow and quiver of arrows, he made his way towards the shady forest.

Robin scanned the ground for signs that might warn of danger. At first there were only deer tracks. But when he came to a broad path, the ground was churned up by footprints and hoof marks. A sizable party had passed this way not long before, and it looked as if they planned to join the main forest road – the road on which Marian Fitzwalter was travelling.

Robin continued down the path. The travellers could not be far ahead, yet he heard no sound. Whatever their purpose, they were going very carefully about their business. He began to feel uneasy.

Soon Robin was close to the road, where it ran through a hollow. Now he could hear faint sounds of movement. Inching forwards, he looked down into the hollow. Almost hidden among the roadside bushes was a group of armed men. Beyond the far side of the road, he could just make out the shape of a horse and rider.

It was an ambush – and Marian Fitzwalter was riding right into it!

*I must stop her!* thought Robin. Circling round, he reached the edge of the road just below the hollow. A moment later, Marian and her servants came into sight.

Robin shouted a warning, but in the same instant an armed horseman crashed through the bushes, blocking Marian's way. Marian's horse reared up in fright as men-at-arms sprang out on all sides to form a semicircle across the road.

His bow at the ready, Robin leapt between Marian and the horseman. 'Clear the way, Knight,' he shouted, 'and let the lady pass freely!'

'Locksley! Saxon dog! Stand aside!' snarled the knight, sword in hand. The next moment he fell from the saddle, an arrow through his heart.

The men-at-arms closed in. In the blink of an eye, Robin loosed three more arrows, and three of the attackers were slain.

Robin fitted another arrow to his bow, but the rest of the men had fled. They dared not face Robin of Locksley, renowned as the most accurate bowman in the Sheriffdom of Nottingham – if not all England.

Marian looked down at the dead knight. 'Roger de Mortmain,' she said. 'One of my family's most bitter enemies!'

'We must hurry now,' said Robin. 'There may be others of de Mortmain's people looking out for you. He had many evil supporters. The

*The men-at-arms closed in*

sooner I bring you to your father, the better.'

It was midday before they came in sight of Malaset Manor, the home of the Fitzwalters. After Marian and her father greeted each other, Robin described what had happened.

'Robin of Locksley,' said Sir Richard Fitzwalter, 'you have done my family a great service. Roger de Mortmain was an evil man. No reward I could offer would be high enough. But you have put yourself in great danger – killing a Knight of the Realm is a grave offence. The High Sheriff of Nottingham is bound to issue a warrant for your arrest. You must flee at once. Go into hiding.'

'No,' replied Robin. 'The Sheriff, or his crony Guy of Gisborne, is more likely to take revenge on me by attacking my people. I must return to Locksley without delay!' And he set off with all speed and urgency towards Locksley Hall.

He was nearing the edge of the woodland and

the open fields when he heard a rustle in the undergrowth. A voice called softly, 'Master! Master Locksley! Over here!'

Robin knew the voice. It was Will Scarlett, a poacher by trade, and no friend to the royal foresters. He was dusty and dishevelled, with blood on his face from a cut cheek.

'You must go no further,' Scarlett said. 'Gisborne's men are lying in wait for you. They say you have committed a terrible crime, and they have laid waste to Locksley.'

'What of my people?' asked Robin anxiously.

'They had some warning,' said Will. 'The families escaped to nearby villages. But four of the men were taken prisoner.'

'Gisborne trusts that I will come to their rescue,' said Robin. 'I won't disappoint him.'

They hurried to the Manor of Locksley – or what was left of Robin's former home. Smoke still rose from the ruins. Stables, cottages and

*'That's far enough, Saxon!'*

barns lay wrecked. The mill smouldered darkly in the distance.

'Mutch the miller's son was taken,' said Will. 'Gilbert the ditcher and Nic the carter, too.'

'How many of Gisborne's men are still there?' asked Robin. 'How are they armed?'

'Just six stayed behind with the prisoners, armed with swords only,' said Will.

Robin thought for a moment. 'Here's what you must do, Will,' he said, and whispered something to him. Will nodded, picked up his bow and slipped away through the trees.

Robin strode across the open ground to the rubble-strewn courtyard of the ruined Hall.

'That's far enough, Saxon!'

A sergeant and two men-at-arms stepped out from behind the burning gable. Robin glimpsed three more, partly hidden by the wall. *All six*, he thought. *Good. The prisoners may be bound, but they are unguarded. Probably close by…*

'Ah, Sergeant!' Robin called. 'Had I known you were visiting, I would have stayed to welcome you to my humble home.'

'Home?' laughed the sergeant. 'You call a murdering Saxon rat's bolt-hole a home?'

'Serving in Gisborne Castle,' replied Robin, 'you must know all about rat holes!'

'Enough talk, Robin of Locksley!' shouted the sergeant. 'You are under arrest, for the heinous crime of murder.'

'And who will arrest *you*?' retorted Robin. 'There has long been a law about burning people's houses…'

'Seize him!' cried the sergeant.

The men-at-arms ran forwards. Robin advanced to meet them, sword in hand. One went down to a thrust through his sword arm. A second reeled back, dazed from the flat of Robin's blade across his neck.

The other men-at-arms rushed to join the

fight. Ash and smoke swirled through the air as Robin fought off the attack. He was greatly outnumbered. Where was Will Scarlett?

Suddenly one of the soldiers screamed and fell, transfixed by an arrow. Men were shouting and charging across the courtyard: Will with his bow, and four other men throwing stones and pieces of wood.

'I have a good Saxon arrow for the man who is last to drop his sword!' shouted Will.

But before anyone could move, Mutch cried, 'Back!' and dragged Robin by the sleeve. The Saxons scrambled clear – and only just in time. With a rumble, the fire-weakened gable of Locksley Hall crashed to the ground. The sergeant and his men-at-arms vanished under a heap of broken stone in a cloud of smoke and ash.

From the edge of the forest, Robin looked back. 'I have nothing now,' he said to the men around him, 'but my sword and my longbow. Locksley is no more. I am Robin the outlaw, and must take my chances where I find them.'

'We are all outlaws,' said Will Scarlett, 'including Hal, here. He brought us warning.'

The man nodded. 'Hal the fletcher,' he said. 'I was delivering arrows to the Gisborne garrison when I heard the orders being given. I came as quickly as I could.' Hal grinned. 'I stole one of Gisborne's horses to speed my way.'

Mutch laughed. 'Here am I, a miller without a mill, *and* an outlaw. My companions? A murderer, a poacher and a horse thief. A merry company indeed!'

Led by Will Scarlett, the small band entered Sherwood Forest. As a poacher, Will knew every secret path and hidden glade. The sun was setting when he called a halt. They were in a wide clearing. A stream flowed nearby. A high rock stood like a watchtower to one side.

*The small band entered Sherwood Forest*

'I suggest we camp here tonight,' said Will.

Nic lit a fire. Will went off with his bow and returned shortly with the carcass of a young stag. 'Tonight we dine on royal venison,' he cried, 'as served at the table of our true and Christian King… Richard the Lionheart.'

'And of his evil brother, John,' said Gilbert.

'But not in such fine company,' laughed Mutch.

They all fetched water from the stream in their hats – all, that is, except Robin.

'I have no hat,' he said, 'only the hood of my jerkin.'

Mutch laughed again. 'Then I would be honoured to share mine with you, Robin o' the Hood!'

'Yes!' cried Will Scarlett. 'Robin of Locksley is dead. Long live our leader – Robin o' the Hood!'

# LITTLE JOHN

*Robin called the men together*

Mutch's nickname for Robin of Locksley stuck – only shortened to 'Robin Hood'. The band of outlaws grew quickly. Some were men of Locksley, like Will Stutely. Others were tradesmen, like Arthur Bland, a tanner from Nottingham. He was outlawed because he had beaten a Norman merchant who had cheated him over some leather.

One day, Robin called the men together. 'There are almost forty of us now,' he said. 'We are all wanted men. So we must be ready to fight for our freedom. We must also fight to defend the poor, the weak and the helpless.'

'But how can we fight?' asked Nic. 'None of us are warriors, and we have no weapons.'

'Then you must learn,' said Robin. 'First you will learn how to fight with quarterstaves. We have a champion in our midst – right, Mutch?'

'I did win a prize at Nottingham Fair,' Mutch confessed, blushing. 'But that's only sport.'

'Not the way I've seen you play!' laughed Hal the fletcher. 'You left ten opponents with very sore heads.'

'Right,' said Robin. 'I appoint Mutch as quarterstaff instructor. Each man will cut an ash staff for himself. Then somehow we must find swords, bows and arrows for us all. We will be a small army, but to keep order we must have rules,' he went on. 'First, our enemies are greed and cruelty.'

'And Normans,' said Will Stutely.

'Not all Normans,' Robin pointed out. 'We can count on several important Normans as friends. The Fitzwalters of Malaset, for instance. There are also many cruel and greedy Saxons. All who travel through Sherwood Forest should be invited to contribute money or goods to help the weak and helpless. And if they don't like the invitation, then they will be, let's say, *persuaded*,' said Robin, grinning.

'I see!' cried Mutch. 'Our first rule: rob the rich to feed the poor! And, as we are poor, we shall also feed ourselves. Very simple, really.'

Robin continued. 'Peasants, farmers, squires, knights, pilgrims and beggars may pass freely, except those whom we know to be villains or troublemakers.'

The outlaws took it in turns to keep watch from a high rock. One morning there was a shout from the lookout.

'Something or someone is moving along the Nottingham road!' he called. 'The birds and wild animals are very disturbed. It may be a company of considerable number!'

'Dick!' Robin called to one of the young outlaws. 'Keep out of sight and find out who is taking the high road to Nottingham.' Within an hour, Dick was back. 'A covered ox cart,' he reported, 'with an armed guard of eight soldiers – four riding in front, and four behind.'

'Supplies for the castle,' said Robin. 'I think we might change that to supplies for Robin Hood and his men!'

———⟫◆⟪———

The slow-moving cart and its escort stopped in a clearing, where the road forked. A charcoal-burner's hut stood by the roadside.

'Hey! Charcoal-burner!' bellowed the captain of the escort. 'Which is the road to Nottingham, peasant?'

There was no reply. The captain dismounted, strode over to the hut, and banged hard on the door. At the same moment, an arrow thudded into the wood, a hair's breadth from his fist. The captain whirled round. A second arrow hit the door on his other side, close to his shoulder. The captain drew his sword and started to shout an order. But a third arrow grazed the top of his helmet, then struck the door above his head.

'I shall give the orders!' called a voice from

*The captain drew his sword*

among the trees. 'You are surrounded. And we have more arrows than you have soldiers!'

There was a stirring in the trees. Half-hidden behind every tree and bush, the soldiers could make out the figure of a man. They knew they were outnumbered many times over.

The mysterious voice gave the orders quickly. The soldiers dismounted and dropped their swords to the ground. Looking fearfully about them, they crowded into the dark, windowless hut. Then the door was closed and wedged shut from outside.

Once the door was secure, Robin and the outlaws came out into the open and uncovered the cart. It was loaded with long, wooden crates.

Hal opened a crate. 'Arrows!' he exclaimed. 'And bows!' There were also swords and sword-belts – all destined for Nottingham Castle.

The outlaws emptied the cart. Two to a crate, they started back to the camp.

Robin and Will Scarlett gathered up the weapons dropped by the escort. 'I believe in telling the truth,' said Robin. 'We did have more arrows. It's just as well that the Normans didn't know that we only had two bows!'

He crossed to the charcoal-burner's hut. 'Robin Hood thanks the Sheriff for his generosity,' he called to his Norman prisoners. 'Long before you manage to break free, we shall be far away. We leave you your cart and horses. It is a long walk from here to Nottingham, and in any case animals and prisoners are too much trouble for us to feed and guard. Goodbye, and safe journey to you all!'

The High Sheriff of Nottingham raged when the news reached him. Prince John was even more furious. 'Robin Hood! Robin Hood! That's all I hear!' he shouted. 'My own stable boys and scullions speak of no one else!'

By training and practising every day, the

outlaws became adept with their new weapons. Soon there were few to equal their mastery at quarterstaff, swordplay and archery.

Grasping landlords and harsh Norman overseers found themselves waylaid on forest roads and persuaded to hand over their money. Gifts of money, food and clothing were often left mysteriously at the doors of cottages in peasant villages.

Some men of the Church, who should have known better, grew fat on the toil of the peasants who worked the Church lands, and increased their rents. One day, Robin and his men had ambushed the Abbey's rent collectors to recover peasants' money. Now they were returning to camp.

The track they were following came out into a broad meadow through which flowed a wide, deep stream. A fallen tree made a bridge.

As usual when crossing open ground, the outlaws were very cautious. Robin went first, hurrying towards the tree bridge. He was just turning to give a signal to the others to follow him, when they heard a loud shout from the far bank.

A tall, burly man stood with one foot on the fallen tree. 'One moment, friend!' he shouted. 'I want to cross!'

'By all means!' Robin called back. 'As soon as I've come over, the way is free for you to cross.'

'No, no!' shouted the tall man. 'I have right of way, as I have already set foot on the bridge. Step aside like a good fellow.' And he laughed and twirled a long staff in front of him.

Robin unslung his bow. 'I do not yield to threats!' he said angrily.

'Then let us dispute it man to man!' cried the other. 'But I am unarmed except for my staff. Bow against quarterstaff is hardly fair.' He laughed again and thumped the end of the staff on the tree trunk.

*The forest echoed to the crack of staves*

Robin laid his bow and quiver on the ground. 'Lend me your quarterstaff, Nic,' he called. The outlaws came out into the open, and Nic tossed Robin his ash staff.

The two men advanced to the middle of the log. Robin's opponent gave a great laugh. 'Now, archer, let's see you *really* fight!'

Robin used all his skill, but he could not land a single blow. Neither could the other, though he was a head taller and had a longer reach than Robin.

The forest echoed to the crack of staves as each man swung and parried. Then Robin slipped and lost his balance. With a resounding splash, he tumbled into the water.

The big man peered into the stream, where Robin's staff floated among the ripples. Robin was nowhere to be seen.

'I hope I haven't drowned your friend,' he said to the outlaws. 'I rather liked him…'

His voice broke off with a yell as Robin, who had surfaced on the other side of the log, grabbed his ankle. Another splash, and the two of them stood up, waist deep, and waded, laughing, to the bank.

Robin pointed to the bridge. 'The road is clear,' he said. 'You may continue on your way now.'

'In a moment,' said the man, 'when I get my breath and empty my boots of water.'

The outlaws crossed to join them. Nic asked the man, 'Where are you bound?'

'To find my cousin,' said the big man. 'I heard he was in these parts. Wanted by the law. Trouble with a cheating Norman leather merchant. Arthur, they call him. Arthur Bland. Perhaps you've heard of him.'

Robin and the outlaws roared with laughter.

'Heard of him? He's one of our company!' said Robin.

'Then you must be Robin Hood!' exclaimed

*Robin and the outlaws roared with laughter*

the big man, joining in the laughter. 'I'm John Little, until recently a cattleman on a farm near Mansfield. I'm in much the same sort of trouble as cousin Arthur – a Norman steward got in the way of my fist! You're not recruiting, by any chance, are you, Master Hood?'

'Well,' grinned Robin, 'we do happen to have a vacancy for a fellow like yourself. You may join us on one condition. We are a merry company and fond of a joke. You will forget that you were ever John Little. From this day, you will be known as *Little John*. Agreed?'

'Agreed,' said the new outlaw. 'Little John I shall be... in name, if not in size or deed!'

Little John became a popular member of the band. None could be down at heart in his company, and he was a strong and fearless fighter. In time, he would become Robin Hood's right-hand man.

# THE SILVER ARROW

One of Robin Hood's friends was a monk, Brother Anselm. Robin once asked him, 'Why not join us here in the forest? Like our king, Richard the Lionheart, we are God-fearing Christians. We need a chaplain.'

Brother Anselm replied, 'No, Robin, my work is with the sick in the Abbey infirmary. However, if you want a man of peace to serve your band, you could do worse than seek Brother Tuck of Copmanhurst. He has upset the Abbot of St Mary's because he refuses to accept a fee for marrying people. Not only that, he usually brings a haunch of venison to the wedding feast – so he is also an enemy of the royal foresters. Another thing,' added Brother Anselm. 'Instead of "Brother", he calls himself by the French title "Friar" – Friar Tuck.'

A few days later, Robin, with Little John and half a dozen others, set off to find Friar Tuck. Near the edge of Copmanhurst Forest they came to a stream. There, holding a fishing line, was a burly man with a shaved head and a monk's habit.

Robin approached him. 'Holy man,' he said, 'I wish to cross the stream. Will you, like good Saint Christopher, carry me?'

'As you wish,' said the monk, leaning over so Robin could climb on his back. He waded into the stream and quickly reached the far bank. 'Now,' said Robin, 'I would be obliged if you would take me back again.'

Without a word of complaint, the monk carefully retraced his steps. But halfway across the stream, he made a sudden move to throw Robin off his back.

Robin gripped hard with his arms and legs. 'Not quite yet, my friend,' he said. 'I prefer to reach the bank dry-shod.'

'As you please,' the monk laughed. As they reached the water's edge, he suddenly dropped

*The monk put Robin flat on the ground*

onto one knee. Robin flew through the air and hit the ground with a thump, but he was on his feet in time to grab the monk in a wrestler's hold.

Robin soon realised that he had met his match as a wrestler. With one skilful throw, the monk put Robin flat on the ground, sat on him and cried, 'Submit?'

'I submit!' replied Robin. 'For a man of the Church you are a fearsome wrestler!'

'We men of God are required to wrestle with Satan. Wrestling with men is good practice,' chuckled the monk.

As they all made their way to the monk's shack, Robin said, 'So you are Friar Tuck!'

'The same,' said Tuck. 'And you, I am certain, are Robin Hood. I'm not sure that an outlaw is fit company for a man of peace.' But he grinned cheekily as he spoke, and fetched mugs and a firkin of ale.

Robin looked round. For a man of peace,

Tuck was well equipped. A sword hung on a wall.

'Will you join us?' Robin asked the Friar.

'I'll think about it,' said Tuck. 'It can be lonely here – except when Gisborne's men come bothering me!'

When the outlaws rose to go, Tuck rose, too. 'I'll accompany you part of the way,' he said.

They had gone barely a mile when Little John said, 'Listen! Someone's in trouble!'

Carried on the breeze came the sound of men shouting, horses neighing and the clash of weapons. They hurried towards the noise, and soon saw a milling crowd of men and horses engaged in battle. Some of the men wore livery and were armed.

'Gisborne's cutthroats!' cried Tuck. 'And my sword left hanging on the wall!' He picked up a stout tree branch and charged down the slope. The outlaws could hardly keep up with him.

One of the attackers was trying to pull a

white-haired man from his horse. Tuck briskly whirled the branch round and sent the attacker spinning.

Taken by surprise, Gisborne's men were quickly overcome. Some fled, others were brought down by well-aimed arrows.

'I'm in your debt,' said the white-haired man. 'I'm Simon of Lincoln. Those villains would have stolen the goods I was taking to Nottingham market.'

One of Simon's people was badly hurt. 'You must rest before continuing,' Robin said. 'Be our guest tonight, and tomorrow we will see you safely to Nottingham.'

———⟶◦⟵———

Next morning, Simon of Lincoln prepared to leave. 'I owe you a great deal, including my life,' he said. 'I must reward you. Most of you could use some new garments. Perhaps this will help.' He took from one of his horses a bolt of fine, dark green woollen cloth. 'This is woven in my own town. There we call it Lincoln green,' he explained.

Escorted by Will Scarlett, Simon and his people went on their way. When Will returned, he had some news.

'Prince John is holding an archery contest,' he said, 'to find the champion bowman of all England. The prize is a silver arrow.'

Little John frowned. 'This is no ordinary contest,' he said. 'Why hold it in a small town like Nottingham? I think Prince John has only one purpose... to lure Robin into a trap.'

'You may be right,' said Robin, 'but I *must* take part. A Saxon champion would be a great thing for the ordinary people – and, better still, a blow to John and his Norman cronies.'

On the day of the contest, the outlaws made their way to Nottingham. Robin wore old, shabby clothes. His face, grimy with wood ash, was hidden by his long, hooded cloak. His hair and beard were uncombed. He looked like a beggar.

Stands had been erected, and the targets were set up on the common land outside the town. Busy stalls sold food and drink. Flags flew over the colourful pavilions of the nobility. Over the largest pavilion flew the standard of the sly Prince John.

Amidst all this splendour, people crowded from far and near, eager to see who would be declared champion. Soldiers of the garrison kept a close watch on the crowd. But the outlaws came in ones and twos, their weapons hidden under their cloaks, so they attracted no attention. Robin went off to report to the marshals.

At last the contest began. There were more than eighty contestants. Steadily they were eliminated until only four were left, including Robin. The targets were removed, and new ones were made ready.

*'That is our man'*

As Little John watched anxiously, there was a tug at his sleeve. 'Master Simon!' he exclaimed.

'You must get away, all of you!' said the merchant. 'Gisborne has a troop of mounted men hidden behind the royal pavilion. He will attack you as soon as you leave.'

Little John looked round for the others. But he could not see them in the crowd – and the final part of the contest was about to begin.

The targets were slender willow wands, set upright in the ground. An arrow that did not strike true would glance off the slippery wood and not count as a hit.

In the royal stand, Prince John and the Sheriff of Nottingham watched the competitors closely for signs that one might be Robin Hood.

'That is our man,' said the prince, pointing.

'Do you mean the beggar, Your Highness?' asked the sheriff.

'No beggar stands so proud in front of his

betters,' said the prince. 'If that is not Robin Hood then I am not John Lackland!'

The first archer prepared to shoot. Thinking quickly, Little John leaned down and whispered to one of his Saxon neighbours, 'They say the tall one is Robin Hood!'

The Saxon whispered excitedly to others around him, and soon the whispers ran all through the crowd: 'Robin Hood? Is it? Yes, surely! It is! It's Robin Hood!'

There was a hush as the first archer loosed an arrow. He missed. So did the second man. There was a gasp as the third archer's arrow grazed the willow wand, but then it too hit the ground.

Now it was the turn of the hooded beggar.

A great roar of applause went up from the crowd as the beggar's arrow split the willow cleanly. Prince John stood up.

'Step forward, archer!' he cried. 'Champion bowman of all England… by a *lucky* shot!'

'Lucky!' cried Robin. In one smooth movement he turned and shot another arrow. It hit the first squarely and split it neatly in two.

The prince sneered. 'I knew you would be unable to resist... *Robin Hood*!'

'Guards!' shouted the sheriff. 'Arrest him!'

But his voice was lost in the crowd's roar. The guards were swept aside by a cheering mob of Saxons. The outlaws pushed their way to Robin; Little John had managed to tell them of Gisborne's trap. As the crowd spilled out from the archery ground, the outlaws were swept along in the confusion.

Tents collapsed, booths overturned and Gisborne saw his carefully planned ambush in ruins. His men-at-arms tried to force their way through the mob, but their horses, startled by the uproar, plunged and reared. When the Saxons began hurling pieces of the wrecked booths, the horsemen backed off.

*It was Guy of Gisborne!*

As the outlaws raced for the forest, they could hear the hoofbeats of six horses, led by Guy of Gisborne, rapidly closing in on them.

Robin, Little John, Mutch and Nic formed a rear guard while the others sprinted for cover. Arrows whizzed all around them, and suddenly Little John went down, wounded in the leg. Mutch ran to his aid, just managing to drag him towards the trees. They were pursued by a single horseman.

Robin raised his bow and shot; the horseman crashed down. It was Guy of Gisborne!

'You missed him!' cried Gilbert in disbelief.

'When the time comes, Guy of Gisborne and Robin of Locksley will meet in combat face to face,' said Robin. 'But now, I still have some unfinished business with Prince John.'

'Prince John?' asked Will Scarlett.

'Yes,' grinned Robin. 'He forgot to present me with my silver arrow!'